To my parents, Bert and Evelyn Goldman, who introduced me to books and reading, and to my brother Jim, for being there

—J. G.

For the new kids in town, Ian and Irina

—F. V. B.

Thank you!
I would like to thank my Charlesbridge family: Randi Rivers, Susan Sherman, Yolanda Scott, and Brent Farmer. Also a huge *gracias* to Dr. Alejandro González Villarroel, Dr. Johannes Neurath, anthropologist Marta Turok, Mtra. Ana Lilia Márquez Valdez, Father Ricardo Robles, Mtra. Yolanda Valdez Jara, Xuno López, Fausto Sandoval Cruz, and Ilan Rabchinskey for taking the time to read the nonfiction information, making comments, and correcting it. Any mistakes that appear were made unintentionally by me.

Published by Charlesbridge
85 Main Street
Watertown, MA 02472
(617) 926-0329
www.charlesbridge.com

Library of Congress Cataloging-in-Publication Data
Goldman, Judy, 1955–
    Whiskers, tails and wings: animal folktales from Mexico / Judy Goldman;
illustrated by Fabricio VandenBroeck.
       p. cm.
    Includes bibliographical references and index.
    ISBN 978-1-58089-372-5 (reinforced for library use)
    ISBN 978-1-60734-617-3 (ebook)
1. Indians of Mexico—Folklore. 2. Tales—Mexico. 3. Animals—Mexico—Folklore.
I. VandenBroeck, Fabricio, 1954– ill. II. Title. III. Title: Animal folktales from Mexico.
F1219.3.F6G65 2012
398.20972—dc23   2012024636

Printed in China
(hc) 10 9 8 7 6 5 4 3 2 1

Illustrations done in acrylics and watercolors on a custom texturized paper
   and then manipulated in Photoshop
Display type set in Mambo by Val Fullard
Text type set in Calisto MT by The Monotype Corporation plc
Color separations by KHL Chroma Graphics, Singapore
Printed in February 2013 by 1010 Printing International Limited
   in Huizhou, Guangdong, China
Production supervision by Brian G. Walker
Designed by Diane M. Earley

Whiskers, Tails & Wings

Animal Folktales from Mexico

Judy Goldman

Illustrated by
Fabricio VandenBroeck

iↄi Charlesbridge

Table of Contents

United States

Seri

Tarahumara

Mexico

Huichol

Triqui

Tseltal

Welcome to Mexico

For thousands of years, storytellers have told legends and folktales. Using vivid gestures and expressive voices, they are like magicians who keep their listeners spellbound.

These legends and folktales speak to the heart and soul of a people. They reflect ancient wisdom and help strengthen the memory and identity of a culture. They pass on beliefs and values. They give meaning to life and help explain the universe. They are also a lot of fun to hear.

Mexico, a fascinating country made up of a unique blend of ancient customs and modern ways, is rich with such tales. Different native groups passed these tales from generation to generation. Though many people know about the Aztecs and the Maya, most have never heard about the other indigenous people of Mexico. Today there are sixty-two different native groups that speak as many languages, plus variations. The animal stories in this book are narrated by five of these groups: the Tarahumara, the Seri, the Huichol, the Triqui, and the Tseltal.

The lifestyles of these indigenous groups vary from member to member: Some continue to live as their ancestors did, while others have modern conveniences in their homes. Some houses are still built with local materials, yet others are constructed with bricks and concrete. Some homes have gas stoves, computers, refrigerators, TVs, beds with mattresses, and telephones, while others are sparsely furnished. Cell phones are used by many. A good number of schools have at least one computer, so students learn how to surf the Internet.

Due to poverty some members of these groups have emigrated to big cities (and even to other countries) seeking work. As a result of being so far from home, they have lost some of their traditions. But others, especially those who still live in small towns and on farms in their native territories, strive to maintain their language, customs, and way of life. They love the land and what it produces. Many dress as their ancestors did, hand-weaving and embroidering fabrics to make their clothes. They create folk art recognized all over the world for its originality and beauty. Telling their stories is also a way of holding on to their traditions.

Many native stories are so old that their origins are lost to time. Some are about gods, heroes, and supernatural creatures. Others are about flowers, trees, and other plants—such as tales about the creation of *maíz,* or corn, the most important crop in Mexico. A lot of stories are about animals, explaining how these creatures came to be and why a native culture holds certain beliefs and traditions.

While many stories were created in Mexico, others have their origins in Spain. Beginning in the eighth century, Spain was under Moorish rule for more than seven centuries. During this period, culture and commerce flourished, and there was a great deal of trade with the Middle East, India, and northern Africa.

Tales were often changed and influenced by other cultures as they traveled back and forth along trade routes. The new stories

Glossary for "Welcome to Mexico!"

maíz (my-EES) [Spanish] corn

began to arrive in what would later be called Mexico when Hernán Cortés and his men conquered it for Spain in 1521.

Soon after the Spanish conquest, people from many countries, like England, China, the Netherlands, and the Philippines, sought out this new land and the opportunities it provided. They brought with them fairy tales and folktales from their native lands. Some stories arrived with African slaves who were brought over to work in the mines and sugar fields. Over time these tales were embellished or mixed with Mexico's existing ones. This created one-of-a-kind stories such as the ones in this book; despite their mixed origins, these stories still captured the essence of each culture that told the tale.

In Mexico it is common to hear people say hospitably, *"Mi casa es tu casa,"* or "My home is your home." So welcome to Mexico, *mi casa,* and enjoy its wonderful stories and the affectionate people who tell them.

Mi casa es tu casa. (MEE KAH-sah ESS TOO KAH-sah) [Spanish] My home is your home.

When Señor Grillo Met Señor Puma

Señor Puma was in a bad mood. He stomped through the forest, looking neither left nor right, much less where he stepped.

Suddenly someone yelled, *"¡Oye, tú!* Watch where you're going! You almost killed me!"

Señor Puma stopped in his tracks. He looked for the source of the voice. Down by Señor Puma's paw was a very annoyed cricket who was shaking his antennae at him. Under normal circumstances Señor Puma would have laughed and gone on his way, but today he was ripe for picking a fight.

"Who cares?" Señor Puma said. "You are so small and weak that you are good for nothing!" With a quick movement of his paw, he flicked Señor Grillo into the weeds.

Señor Grillo was even angrier than before. He picked himself up and shouted, "It is a shame that you should treat me this way. *¡Eres un cobarde!"*

With a roar, Señor Puma yelled, "You cannot call me a coward and get away with it! This is war! Prepare your army, and tomorrow we will meet in the meadow near the shore of the lake. I will get rid of you and your kind."

Señor Puma stalked off to recruit his army. Through the forest he went, roaring and calling at the top of his lungs, "Come, *hermanos,* your king calls you to arms!"

The first volunteers were two bears he spotted among the trees. They were soon joined by two more pumas and five ferocious bobcats. Señor Puma also enlisted a family of foxes, some skunks, and three nasty snakes. Then he spent the rest of the day drilling his army until they were ready to fight.

Meanwhile, Señor Grillo sat quietly under a tree, thinking about how he could win the upcoming battle. After a while he left to arrange everything.

Early the next morning, when the sun was beginning to splash the sky with color, Señor Puma and his troops arrived at the battleground.

"Halt!" Señor Puma ordered, looking over the combat zone.

All was quiet.

The only odd thing he spotted were several yellow gourds dotting the field.

Señor Puma snorted and said, "Why, the little coward didn't show up."

Then he saw a movement.

Señor Grillo was there after all, standing at the other end of the field.

Señor Puma snickered and said, "That silly insect is by himself! Does he think he's going to beat us by throwing gourds? Foolish creature, how can he possibly win? Ha! This is going to be the shortest war in history!"

The other animals laughed so hard that they fell to the ground, whooping, slithering, and shaking. After a few minutes, they stood up and, still laughing and wiping their eyes, took their positions.

With a snarl, Señor Puma gave the order to begin the battle. The animals howled and rushed at the lone cricket, ready to crush him into the ground.

But at that moment, a multitude of crickets jumped up from behind the gourds and whipped off their tops. Señor Grillo's army poured from the hollow gourds—hundreds of angry wasps hovering above his head like a storm cloud.

When Señor Puma saw the buzzing swarm, he skidded to a stop. "Run for your lives!" he yelled.

All was confusion as the animals in front stopped in their tracks and the ones behind plowed into them. Legs, tails, and bodies jumbled together.

Howling at the tops of their lungs, they untangled themselves and turned tail, running as fast as they could, with Señor Puma sprinting at the head of his vanquished army.

Even though they raced as swiftly as possible, tripping over stones and roots and crashing into trees and each other, the wasps soon caught up with them. Señor Puma shouted, "Run to the lake. Only there will we be safe!"

As soon as they reached the water, the animals dove into the lake. There they stayed until the wasps decided that they had had enough. Only then did Señor Puma's army crawl home to lick its wounds.

That night Señor Grillo and his army had a grand party to celebrate their victory. There was food and drink and song, and, as a special treat, Señor Grillo composed an epic poem narrating their triumph, and then he set it to music on the spot.

Since then crickets sing that song every night to remember Señor Grillo's victory over Señor Puma.

And pumas are very careful not to upset them.

The Tarahumara

Small, delicate crickets and strong, swift pumas have, through the centuries, adapted to their rugged homeland. They have become one with it because only those who are quick and clever will survive in a place that, while being beautiful, can also be harsh. The same can be said about the Tarahumara.

The Tarahumara call themselves the Rarámuri. They live in the northern part of Mexico in the Sierra Tarahumara mountains, a range that is part of the vast Sierra Madre Occidental. The Sierra Tarahumara makes its way through the states of Durango, Chihuahua, and Sonora. It has nine major canyons, some of which—at their lowest parts—are deeper than the Grand Canyon! One of them, the Cañon del Cobre, or Copper Canyon, is a common name for the whole area.

The Sierra Tarahumara is divided into two regions. The Low Tarahumara, where the Yaqui, Mayo, and Fuerte rivers flow through the canyons, is always warm and its trees are full of mangoes and oranges. The High Tarahumara has craggy peaks that prop up the clouds, thick forests, deep ravines, plateaus, and the Basaseachi and Piedra Volada waterfalls, the two highest in the country. Winters here are snowy, cold, and windy.

Fertile land can be hard to find in the High Tarahumara, so the Tarahumara's small homes—built of stone or wood—are scattered among the peaks and valleys. Usually there is very little furniture in each home, generally a few benches and some blanket-covered wooden platforms on which people sleep. During the cold season, some Tarahumara take their goats and a few basic belongings to a warmer location. If they can't lodge with relatives, they

track. Their fitness and training are shaped by where they live and the chores they do. They can be outside all day, walking and running, as they take care of their flocks of goats. Some children walk nine or ten hours to get to school, where they board during the week, and then walk the same distance back home on the weekend. Sooner or later walking leads to running.

The main sporting events of the Tarahumara are races among competing teams. Men take part in the *rarajípari,* a race during which they kick a wooden ball. Women race while throwing an *ariweta,* a hoop made of woven branches, with a stick. In both races neither the ball nor the hoop can be touched with the hands. A true team effort, the races are run through the mountains along rough paths for distances that range from a few miles up to one hundred miles—all for entertainment. Some

might stay in caves where the walls are decorated with paintings created by their ancestors. Other Tarahumara are more nomadic, traveling around with their flocks of goats on a constant basis.

The name Rarámuri means "those who run on light feet." For them, running is living. They run for hours at a steady pace over steep and tough terrain without stopping. They think nothing of running to a nearby town and back again the same day . . . even if the total distance is dozens of miles. They usually run barefoot or wear only their simple leather sandals.

Children prepare to become long-distance runners from a very young age. They don't have a coach or run on a

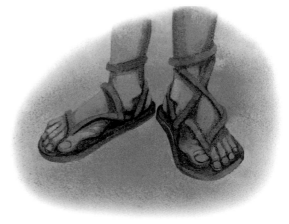

competitions take place over several days and nights without stopping. Teammates encourage the runners by yelling, "¡*Weriga!* Faster!" They are so good at running that it's said that long ago some men hunted deer, wild turkeys, and rabbits by chasing them until the animals died of exhaustion!

To survive this rugged environment and lifestyle, the Tarahumara developed into tough and sturdy people. They also have a strong sense of kinship— much like Señor Grillo and the other insects of this story. Even Señor Puma depended on his friends to help him!

Because families are so isolated

Glossary for "When Señor Grillo Met Señor Puma"

¡Eres un cobarde! (EH-rehs OON koh-BAR-deh) [Spanish] You are a coward!

hermanos (ehr-MAH-nohs) [Spanish] brothers

grillo (GREE-yoh) [Spanish] cricket

¡Oye, tú! (OH-yeh TOO) [Spanish] Hey, you!

señor (SEN-yore) [Spanish] mister

Glossary for "The Tarahumara"

ariweta (ah-ree-WET-ah) [Rarámuri] A hoop made from woven branches. As Tarahumara women race, they throw the *ariweta* with a stick.

Basaseachi (ba-sah-seh-AH-chee) [Rarámuri, "place of coyotes" also "waterfall"] The second highest waterfall in Mexico; also a beautiful princess who flung herself into the abyss after her four suitors, who completed hard tasks planned by her father in order to win her hand, died during the fifth task. Her father turned her body into a waterfall so that she would be immortal.

Cañon del Cobre (kan-NYON del KOH-breh) [Spanish] a canyon in the Sierra Tarahumara that gives its name to the whole range; also Copper Canyon

Chihuahua (chee-WAH-wah) [Spanish] a state in Mexico

Durango (doo-RAWN-goh) [Spanish] a state in Mexico

from the rest of their people, social occasions are few and far between. So any excuse to get together, such as building a home or harvesting a crop, is cause for celebration. People from other *rancherías* gather, and a host family offers a *tesgüinada,* a festivity where everyone relaxes and has a good time while drinking *tesgüino,* a beer made of fermented corn.

Perhaps Señor Grillo started this tradition when he got together with his friends to celebrate their victory over Señor Puma?

Fuerte (FWEHR-teh) [Spanish, "strong"] a river located in the Low Tarahumara

Mayo (MY-yoh) [Spanish] a river located in the Low Tarahumara; also a native group that lives in Sonora; also the month of May

Piedra Volada (pee-EH-drah voh-LAH-dah) [Spanish, "projecting rock"] the highest waterfall in Mexico

rancherías (ran-cheh-REE-as) [Spanish] farms

rarajípari (rah-rah-HEE-pah-ree) [Rarámuri] a race in which teams of men kick a ball over a distance of up to one hundred miles

Rarámuri (rah-RAH-moo-ree) [Rarámuri, "those who run on light feet"] the native people of the Sierra Tarahumara: see also *Tarahumara*

Tarahumara (tah-rah-oo-MAH-rah) [Spanish] name given to the Rarámuri by the Spanish conquerors

tesgüinada (tez-gwee-NAH-dah) [Spanish] communal activity, such as building a house or harvesting a crop, where *tesgüino* is drunk

tesgüino (tez-GWEE-noh) [Spanish] beer made from fermented corn

Sierra Madre Occidental (see-EH-rah MAH-dreh OCK-see-den-tawl) [Spanish] mountain range that runs through the western part of Mexico

Sonora (soh-NOH-rah) [Spanish] a state in Mexico

weriga (WEH-ree-gah) [Rarámuri] faster

Yaqui (YAH-kee) [Spanish] a river in the Low Tarahumara; also a native group that lives in Sonora

A Seri Tale

Mosni's Search

Many, many ages ago, when everything was still new, Hant Caai, the god of creation, sang the sky and the waters into being.

The sky blanketed the heavens. During the day it was dotted with clouds and lit by the sun. At night it was illuminated by thousands of stars and the moon.

Below the sky the sea covered all. Unlike the sky, which was empty of any living being, the sea was overflowing with life. Hant Caai had sung and created many wonderful creatures of all shapes, colors, and sizes to glide in its shallows, dart around its reefs, and hide in its depths.

One day Hant Caai decided it was time to sing the earth into being. To do so he needed sand from the very bottom of the sea. It was so far away that not even he, who had created it, could now reach it.

Hant Caai called on all the sea creatures. Soon whales, octopi, shrimp, eels, sharks, jellyfish, and many, many others gathered around him.

Among them was Mosni, the sea turtle.

The god told them about his need and asked for someone to swim to the bottom of the sea and bring back the sand. "The journey will be long, hard, and dangerous," he warned.

Many were scared and slunk back to their homes. Those who stayed begged to be chosen, each one boasting that he or she was the finest or the fastest or the strongest swimmer.

In a sudden lull, Mosni raised her flipper to volunteer, but the others laughed. "You are too clumsy," they said. "You will never make it." So she swam to the edge of the crowd.

The first chosen was the sea snail, because she said she could bring back the sand inside her shell. She streaked down as fast as she could, her foot propelling her. After a while she stopped to rest. All of a sudden, she noticed she was alone . . . there was nothing nearby, just a huge amount of water above her head and an even bigger amount below. She floated a few seconds more, and then she got so scared that her eyes almost popped out of their tentacles.

"*¡Ayyy!*" she squeaked, and she bolted to the first coral reef she found. There she hid in a cave, too ashamed to leave.

When the sea snail didn't return, the triggerfish volunteered. He said he could bring the sand back in his strong mouth. He swam down and down, but he hadn't gone far when he saw some juicy sea urchins clinging to a rock. His stomach grumbled. The triggerfish thought, *First I will eat something. I must eat to have energy, right? Then I'll get the sand!*

Except that he never did get the sand, because every time he was about to dive, he found something else to eat.

When the triggerfish didn't come back, the seal offered her services. She dove into the water with a whoop. Then she swam down, down, and down, until she bumped into a bunch of her cousins.

"Come play hide-and-seek with us!" they said. The seal forgot everything else and joined the fun. She did not return.

Finally Hant Caai addressed patient Mosni.

He asked, "Can you help me?"

Mosni simply said, "Yes."

Mosni dove into the depths of the waters. Down, down, down, and down she swam—using her front flippers like wings, steering with her rear flippers—around, over, and under obstacles; escaping from creatures that wanted to eat her; stopping to rest only when she was exhausted. Overhead the sun and the moon disappeared and came out so many times that Hant Caai and all the creatures were sure that Mosni had failed. . . .

Until one day Mosni poked her head out of the water. "I'm back," she said, but her face was sad.

"I'm sorry," Mosni said, a tear dripping from her eye. "When I reached the bottom I grabbed the sand in my flippers. But the closer I got to the surface, the more the sand scurried out. Now I have only a few grains left."

But Hant Caai said, "Well done, Mosni. Those few grains of sand are more than enough."

Taking the sand into his hands, he sprinkled it on the surface of the water and sang.

Little by little the grains of sand multiplied and spread. Soon they formed golden beaches. Then the beaches stretched out, farther and farther back, and became the desert. Cacti of different shapes and sizes and trees sprouting green leaves appeared a while later. Beyond, the first mountains reached to the sky.

The first creature who was allowed to walk on the new land was Mosni.

The Seri

Although Spanish invaders named them the Seri, these notably tall people call themselves the Comcáac, meaning "the people." They are a very small native group that has lived where the sea, the sky, and the desert meet, for at least two thousand years. Before the Spanish arrived, the Seri were nomadic, living off the land and sea. Like Mosni, they were very brave. Even the conquerors were unable to completely control them.

Today the Seri live mainly in an area granted to them by the Mexican government three decades ago. Their

territory includes Punta Chueca and El Desemboque, two towns on the coast of Sonora, and Isla Tiburón, the largest island of Mexico. Though they used to live on the island, it is now a wildlife refuge and home to mule deer, white-tailed deer, and bighorn sheep. The Seri are still dedicated to fishing. They are skilled navigators and have a deep understanding of the waters of the Sea of Cortez (known, in Mexico, as the Mar de Cortés or Golfo de California) and the desert sands of Sonora.

Most Seri speak Spanish but prefer to use their own language. Known as Cmique Iitom, it's difficult and few people outside of the tribe speak it. It is used for chatting, telling stories of their gods and heroes—such as "Mosni's Search"—and for calling children in at night. It is also used for singing.

Songs, such as the ones that Hant Caai used to create the world, are very important to the Seri. They are an essential part of their life and traditions. There are different types of songs, such as those of war, those of mourning, and lullabies. Some are sung to make a woman fall in love with a man. Others are sung to the wind and the rain. There are also many songs that tell about the animals of the sea and land.

Songs and dances are done in multiples of four. The Seri believe that the number four is sacred. This is why the majority of Seri celebrations take place over four days and four nights.

Celebrations are organized for fun so that the spirits are happy and bring good luck. The only one with a fixed date is New Year's Day, which coincides with the new moon in July—a time when the *pitahayas* are in bloom, the Pleiades appear in the sky, and the Seri universe begins a new cycle. Everyone dresses in colorful clothes. Food is abundant. The people ask the gods to bless them and bring rain. The ritual *pascola* is performed by a man who, dancing on a wooden platform that echoes his steps, is accompanied by the music of a metal rattle and the voice of a singer.

Years ago the Seri used face paint on a daily basis. Now only the women paint their faces, and only on ceremonial occasions, such as when young girls become adolescents. From little girls to grandmothers, they use delicate patterns of dots, stripes, flowers, leaves, and other designs. Sea turtles are so important to the Seri that, to honor them, sometimes they will also paint their shells with red, white, and blue paint.

Sea turtles are also closely entwined in the Seri's dreams, songs, and stories. Mosni is a leatherback turtle. The Seri, who call leatherback turtles *mosnipol,* believe that they are one of

17

Glossary for "Mosni's Search"

¡ay! (AYE) [Spanish] an exclamation of surprise or fright

Hant Caai (ANT KYE) [Cmique Iitom] the god of creation

Mosni (MOHS-nee) [Cmique Iitom] Many types of sea turtles are broadly
called *moosni* by the Seri; the leatherback turtle is called *mosnípol*
(mohs-NEE-pohl).

Glossary for "The Seri"

*(The ' found in some of the pronunciations listed below stands for a short pause,
as in "uh-oh.")*

Cmique Iitom (kwih-KEH EE-tom) [Cmique Iitom] language spoken by the
Seri

Comcáac (kom-KAH'ACK) [Cmique Iitom, "the people"] name by which
the Seri call themselves; see also *Seri*

El Desemboque (EL des-em-BOH-keh) [Spanish] a town in Sonora, Mexico

18

their people and that they understand them when they sing. This turtle is also honored because Mosni helped Hant Caai create the world. If a leatherback turtle appears near the Seri's boats, they do not capture or eat it. Instead they sing to it and invite it into the boat. Once on land they hold a four-day celebration. They decorate the turtle with traditional designs, sing and dance in its honor, and then return it to the sea.

With the exception of the leatherback turtle, other sea turtles were once an important part of the Seri's diet. They are now eaten just on special occasions. The Seri can only hunt a turtle for ceremonial purposes, and then only with government permission. In fact, the young people of El Desemboque now protect sea turtles and their eggs. Groups patrol the beaches when the turtles come to lay their eggs. Later, when the eggs hatch, these groups help the hatchlings reach the sea.

In this way the Seri are trying to make sure that Mosni and other turtles continue to swim in these waters.

Isla Tiburón (EEZ-lah tee-boo-ROHN) [Spanish] an island where the Comcáac once lived, which is now a wildlife refuge

Mar de Cortés (MARH deh Cor-TES) [Spanish] a sea that separates the Baja California peninsula from the Mexican mainland; also the Gulf of California; also the Sea of Cortez

mosnípol (mohs-NEE-pohl) [Cmique Iitom] leatherback turtles

pascola (pass-KOH-lah) [Spanish] ritual dance performed by a man who, dancing on a wooden platform that echoes his steps, is accompanied by music from a metal rattle and a singer

pitahaya (pee-TAH-yah) [Spanish] a type of cactus commonly found in the Sonoran Desert

Punta Chueca (POON-tah choo-EH-kah) [Spanish] a town in Sonora, Mexico

Seri (SEH-ree) [Spanish] once a nomadic native group, today they live along the coast of Sonora; see also *Comcáac*

Tlacuache's Tail

Tlacuache the opossum had agile hands and a quick mind, but it was his bushy tail that was his pride and joy. He was a peaceful creature who got along with everyone except people. He kept out of their way, since they were cruel to him.

In that long-ago time, people didn't know what it was like to be warm except when the sun shone. Their homes were cold, and what they ate was raw. They prayed to their gods to send them something with which to warm themselves.

One night, while he was up in a tree, Tlacuache saw a flash of light streak from the sky. It landed on some dry branches and caught on—first a spark, then a crackle, and soon the brightness danced from branch to branch.

He watched the people gather around the whirling brightness. One woman put out her hands and said, "This feels like a day when the Sun God is shining." But when a man touched Bright Thing and yelped, everyone ran away.

Except Old Woman. She stayed behind, and only Tlacuache heard her say, "I'm sure you are a gift from the gods."

She gathered many branches and took them to her hut, stacking them to the ceiling. Then she made a small pile in the middle of the floor.

Old Woman went back to Bright Thing and picked up a branch on which it danced. She returned to her hut and thrust Bright Thing into the heap of branches on the floor. It leaped and whirled until Old Woman's home was as warm as a sunny day.

The next morning Tlacuache saw the people gather around a pile of ashes. "We were fools," Headman said. "The gods answered our prayers, but we did not recognize it."

"I think Old Woman has it," a child said. "Last night I saw something shiny peeking out of her house."

Everybody ran to Old Woman's hut. Headman asked her to give him some of Bright Thing. "No, it's mine!" she yelled. No matter how much Headman pleaded, she wouldn't budge.

For several days the people tried to get Bright Thing, but Tlacuache saw Old Woman chase them all away. She spent her days and nights feeding branches to Bright Thing to keep it happy. Once in a while she would nod off, and then she would wake up with a start, ever suspicious someone was trying to steal Bright Thing.

One evening Tlacuache approached Headman and said, "I can help you."

"How can such a puny creature help us?" Headman asked. "Go away before I kick you."

Tlacuache insisted. "I'll bring you Bright Thing if you promise that you and your people will never bother or hunt me again."

Headman was so very desperate to have Bright Thing that he agreed.

"Have your people pile up dry branches." Tlacuache said. "I have seen that it likes to eat wood."

Along the way to Old Woman's hut, Tlacuache gathered several ripe *tunas,* the fruit of the cactus. When he reached her home, he poked his head through the door and asked, "May I come in?"

"No!" she yelled. "You've only come to steal Bright Thing."

"No, no," Tlacuache said, creeping closer. "I brought you some sweet, juicy *tunas.* You must be hungry."

"Go away! You want to trick me, just like all the others."

"Why should I help people?" Tlacuache asked. "The only thing I get from them is pain. I'll give you the fruit if you let me sleep near the warmth tonight. In the morning I'll bring more branches."

Old Woman glanced at the dwindling stack of branches and the little bit of food she had left. She then looked at the *tunas* and finally agreed that Tlacuache could stay.

While Old Woman gobbled the *tunas*, Tlacuache pretended to sleep, keeping one eye slightly open. After a while Old Woman started to nod off. Though she tried to keep her eyes open, soon she was snoring.

Tlacuache picked up a branch and inched closer to Bright Thing. He was about to invite it to step onto the branch when . . .

"You tricky creature!" Old Woman yelled. "I'll never let you get away!" She sprang up to chase him.

As Tlacuache ran, Bright Thing jumped onto his tail. Tlacuache yelped in pain but continued to run.

Old Woman finally cornered him. With a nasty laugh, she reached out to catch him. Tlacuache lunged and bit her hand. As she let out a piercing scream, Tlacuache escaped.

Over the cold ground he raced toward the people's village, while Bright Thing whirled on his tail and lit the night sky.

In the center of the village, Tlacuache threw himself upon the huge pile of branches that the people had gathered. Bright Thing jumped onto the dry wood. Eager hands added more branches, and soon Bright Thing transformed into an army of Bright Things, all dancing and crackling.

Tlacuache leaped off and rolled on the ground, trying to get Bright Thing off his tail. The people tried to help. A woman stomped on his tail, but nothing happened. A man blew on it, but that made Bright Thing leap higher. Finally, Headman threw water on Tlacuache's tail. With a smoky hiss, Bright Thing disappeared.

Tlacuache cradled his tail. He cried when he saw that there wasn't even one little hair left on it! Then he ran away and hid. He didn't hear Headman order his people to never bother Tlacuache again. And he didn't hear that Old Woman had been banished to a cold, dark cave for a week.

Tlacuache nursed his tail. He didn't poke his nose out of his home, even though people came to check on him.

One day his stomach growled, and so he decided it was time to leave his home. He climbed a tall tree and saw a juicy, plump caterpillar on the limb just above his head. He stretched and, just as his fingertips were about to touch his lunch, he slipped. Without thinking, he whipped his bald tail around the limb and found himself hanging upside down.

A grin spread across his face. He was so happy that he swung from the limb for a long, long time.

And to this day *tlacuaches* have no hair on their tails, but it doesn't bother them at all.

The Huichol

This tale is told by the Huichol, who are also known as the Wixaritari. They speak Huichol or Wixaritari, which are part of the Uto-Aztecan language family. Nahuatl, the tongue spoken by the ancient Aztecs and their descendants, also belongs to this family. That is why some words are similar in these languages.

Tlacuache, meaning "opossum," comes from the Nahuatl word *tlacuatzin.* It means "the one who eats everything." Opossums live in cities and rural areas from North America to Argentina. These courageous, agile animals are the only New World marsupials (mammals that have pockets in which they nurture and protect their young). Opossums are very clever and will play dead when they feel they are in danger. Many people in Mexico also believe that *tlacuaches* can be reborn.

The Huichol live mainly in Jalisco, Nayarit, Durango, and Zacatecas. These regions are mostly dry. Many of the Huichol live in remote *ranchos,* where several simple homes, called *ki,* are situated around a shared patio. Traditional houses usually consist of one room and have no windows and only one door. The Huichol raise cattle and take care of the *coamil,* or cornfield, where *maíz,* chilies, beans, and squash are planted for their personal use.

Just like Headman does when he tries to get Bright Thing for his people, the Huichol take their obligations to the community seriously. Their communal assembly meets at least four

25

is held up by two pine posts, which represent the cosmic trees that hold up the sky. Each of the smaller temples around the *tukipa* honors the Huichol's most important gods, such as Our Grandfather, the god of fire, and Our Mother, the goddess of the morning sky.

Once a year, after the harvest, the *jicareros* (men and women who act as

times a year. All male heads of *ranchos* and all single adult men and women must attend. The assembly solves community problems and names people to special jobs. It is lead by prominent elders, known as shamans, who hold their job for life. Shamans are known as "those who know how to dream."

Religious rituals take place in the *tukipa,* a ceremonial center surrounded by several smaller temples that are situated around a circular plaza. The main temple is called a *tuki.* Its thatched roof

26

caretakers for the temples) make a pilgrimage, along with many Huichol, including children, to Wirikuta, which is located in the desert of San Luis Potosí in central Mexico. The Huichol believe this is where the sun and the world were created and where their gods live. In Wirikuta the Huichol sing, dance, and pray for fine crops and for the good health of their people and animals. They also make offerings to their ancestors, who sacrificed themselves to make the sun, the world, and all that is in it. It is their belief that the pilgrimage saves the universe from disorder.

Years ago the journey was done on foot, along the Road of Grandfather Fire, and so it could take up to two months to start the pilgrimage and then return home. Today people can drive part of the way, and so it only takes about a week to complete. Each Huichol is expected to make this pilgrimage at least five times during their lifetime.

In Wirikuta they also gather a cactus called peyote, which is used only by a select few and only during their mystical ceremonies. They believe that the plant is the footprint and heart of the sacred deer who, according to legend, led their ancestors to the place where the sun first came out. They also

believe that the dreams produced by peyote opens their hearts in order for them to see better. According to their myths, their ancestors became gods after having these dreams. Once the *jicareros* have their own visions, they become shamans and singers. Many are gifted storytellers who bring to life tales about their gods and ancestors as well as stories of the animals—such as eagles, snakes, deer, scorpions, buzzards, and opossums—that live in the area.

The Huichol are also known for the art they produce. A yarn painting known as *nierika,* which means "the gift of sight," is usually a representation of their dreams, stories, and legends. A *nierika* is believed to be a true sacred vision of the secret universe of their ancestors, as well as a magical door between worlds. It is only made by a *mara'kame,* a shaman who has been initiated and can communicate with

Glossary for "Tlacuache's Tail"

(The "tl" is pronounced by putting the tongue behind the upper teeth.)

tlacuache (tla-COOWAH-cheh) [Nahuatl] opossum

tunas (TOO-nahs) [Spanish] fruits of the cactus; also called prickly pears

Glossary for "The Huichol"

(The ' found in some of the pronunciations listed below stands for a short pause, as in "uh-oh.")

coamil (koah-MEEL) [Spanish] cornfield

Huichol (wee-CHOL) [Spanish] a native group of Mexico that lives in Jalisco, Nayarit, Durango, and Zacatecas; see *Wixaritari*

Jalisco (ha-LEES-koh) [Spanish] a state in Mexico

jicareros (hee-kah-REHR-ros) [Spanish] men and women who act as caretakers for the Huichol temples

ki (KEE) [Wixaritari] house; also roof

mara'kame (mah-rah'KAH-meh) [Wixaritari] a shaman who can communicate with the gods: also *mara'acame*

the sun, fire, and *maíz*. He or she is the only one who can be in touch with the gods.

Making a *nierika* is a skill that is passed on from generation to generation. In order to keep the tradition alive, children are taught how to make simple *nierikas*. If one of them becomes a shaman, he or she might become a fine maker of true *nierikas* and a storyteller, telling tales such as "Tlacuache's Tail."

Nahuatl (NAH-wah-tl) [Nahuatl] part of the Uto-Aztecan language family; spoken by the ancient Aztecs and passed down to their descendants

Nayarit (nah-yah-REET) [Spanish] a state in Mexico

nierika (knee'eh-REEK-ah) [Wixaritari, "the gift of sight"] a yarn painting; considered a sacred vision of the Huichol ancestors' universe as well as a magical door between worlds

peyote (peh-YOH-teh) [Spanish] a type of cactus used in Huichol mystical ceremonies

ranchos (RAWN-chohs) [Spanish] farms

San Luis Potosí (SAHN loo'EES poh-toh-SEE) [Spanish] a state in Mexico

tuki (TOO-kee) [Wixaritari] a temple

tukipa (too-KEY-pah) [Wixaritari] ceremonial center

Wirikuta (vee-ree-COO-tah) [Wixaritari] a sacred place located in the desert of San Luis Potosí

Wixaritari (veeks-ah-ree-TAH -ree) [Wixaritari] name that the Huichol use to call themselves; also the language spoken by the Huichol; see *Huichol*

Zacatecas (sah-kah-TEH-kahs) [Spanish] a state in Mexico

A Triqui Tale

Ouch!

A long time ago, the God of Creation made Man and Woman and gave them the new earth to live on.

Man and Woman lived very much at ease. They slept under a blanket of moonbeams and had only to raise a hand to pick a sweet banana or bend down to drink cool water from a clear spring.

They became quite lazy.

The God of Creation was worried. He did not care to see Man and Woman waste the day doing nothing. He decided that if he couldn't make them change their ways, he would have to destroy these two creatures. Yet they had been difficult to make, and he didn't want to have to start all over.

For many days and nights the god pondered this problem. Meanwhile Man and Woman became even idler than before. Now all they did was lie under a fruit tree and sleep most of the day. If they were hungry, they shook the tree, held out their hands, and waited for a sweet, ripe *mamey* or a tart *guayaba* to fall to them.

At last the god had an idea. He mixed dirt and water and made a thick paste. With it he formed several little balls. To each he added curly vines, twigs, minute chips of obsidian, flower petals, and leaves. Then he named them and set them to dry.

He was tidying up when he found a small piece of paste and, as an afterthought, formed a ball so tiny that it was practically invisible. It was so tiny that the god didn't even give it a name.

Once the balls had dried, the god breathed on them and watched them wake to life. Wings fluttered, antennae uncurled, legs stretched. The creatures buzzed. They scurried, they whirled, they droned! They were so thrilled to be in the new world that they whizzed round and round the god until he was quite dizzy.

31

Once they calmed down, the creatures gathered around the god. He explained what they had to do. Each was so eager to be first that they shoved and jostled one another, trying to attract the god's attention. Even the tiniest one bounced up and down as if it had a wound-up coil in its body.

The god smiled at its antics but shook his head. "You are much too small," he said. Instead he pointed to a buzzing creature and called out, "¡Mosco! Make Man and Woman move so they start to work."

Mosco buzzed around Man's head, darting in and out, up and down. Man yelled, *"¡Lárgate!"* and swatted Mosco so hard that it was almost squashed against the ground.

When the god saw this, he looked over the remaining group. Again each creature clamored to be chosen, the tiniest thing bouncing even higher than before. But the god ignored it and made his choice, calling, "¡Piojo!"

Piojo scampered all over Woman and tickled her. Again and again she slapped here and there until she caught it. *"¡Lárgate!"* she yelled, and flicked Piojo away so hard that it fainted.

The god sent one creature after another—Araña, Abeja, Mariposa, Avispa, and Hormiga—but nothing helped: Man and Woman just knocked each one away and then went back to sleep.

The god looked over the creatures he had made. The wounded ones were a sorry sight. Only the tiniest one was left, now bouncing so high that it almost reached the god's waist.

With a big sigh, he said, "Go!"

The God of Creation watched it set off toward Man and Woman. Holding his breath, the god waited for something to happen. Man and Woman slept undisturbed.

After a few minutes, he frowned, shook his head, and thought,

There is nothing to be done. . . . I will have to get rid of these creatures.

The god raised his arms to the sky. Just as he was about to destroy Man and Woman, he stopped.

Woman had jumped up!

"Something bit my rump!" she screeched.

Man sprang up!

"Mine, too!" he wailed, rubbing his behind.

"What is it?" Woman asked as she watched a red spot appear. "It hurts, it itches, it stings."

"I don't know," Man responded, "but let's find it and get rid of it, just like all the others." They searched here and there but found nothing. After a while Man yawned and said, "I'm sure it's gone. Come, let's rest a while longer." He stretched out under a tree and closed his eyes. Woman lay by his side.

A few quiet seconds passed until . . . Man and Woman jumped up again.

"It's back!" Man yelled, rubbing his leg.

Woman yelped and slapped her arm.

Each time they tried to lie down the same thing happened. So they got to their feet.

The god was delighted with the tiniest creature. He rewarded it with the ability to jump much higher than any other creature of its size. The god then named it Pulga.

From that day on, Man and Woman behaved as the god intended them to—they worked, built a home, planted crops, and brought up a family. If after a hard day's work they rested or played, then they were able to do so undisturbed. But if they tried to spend the whole day lying under a tree, Pulga would appear out of nowhere and remind them of the work to be done.

This is how fleas came to be.

The Triqui

The Triqui call themselves "the people of the complete language." They live in the western part of the southeastern state of Oaxaca in a region known as the Mixteca—"the land of the clouds." They have resided there for several centuries.

The Triqui are hard-working people. Though their homes are scattered, they occupy two main settlements. One is San Andrés Chicahuaxtla. In this high zone, fog covers the ground, hides the trees, and wraps itself around the mountains. It's hard to grow food, since there isn't much running water available and the surrounding terrain is rough. The other town is San Juan Copala. This low zone has warmer weather, abundant water, and fertile land.

Triqui homes can be modern or traditional or a blend of both. Traditional ones usually consist of only one room. The walls are made of tree trunks or mud mixed with rocks, and the roofs are thatched. The women build cooking fires on the floor. There is very little furniture and people sleep on the dirt floor atop *petates,* woven palm mats that are rolled up during the day. Other homes are made of wood or brick and have cement floors and modern conveniences.

Family is very important to the Triqui. They live in extended clans made up of parents, their unmarried children, and their married sons' families. Elders are treated with great respect. Babies and toddlers are pampered, because the Triqui believe that it's bad to let them cry. Once children reach school age, they are expected to obey, do chores, and learn from observing their parents at work.

Work, which usually starts at dawn and ends at sunset, is divided in a traditional manner. Women weave, prepare

meals, fetch water, clean the house, and take care of the children and poultry. Men farm, gather firewood, care for the domestic animals, and are in charge of political and religious matters. Both men and women sell pottery, textiles, woven bags, and handmade toys on market day.

On market day Chicahuaxtla is awash in an ocean of red. This is because most of the women and girls wear a bright red *huipil*. A *huipil,* which can take four to six months to make, is a traditional long, loose blouse that reaches the ankles. Triqui women have been wearing them since before the Spanish conquest.

Nimble-fingered Triqui women are master weavers. One of their responsibilities is to pass this art on to their daughters. Time spent weaving is time spent in close conversations that establish strong bonds between women, especially between mothers and daughters. The vivid colors and forms that are woven into the textiles represent their history and their vision of the world. Their daily life is hard and many times silent, and weaving is sometimes the only way their voices are heard.

Thanks to one tiny insect long ago, the God of Creation did not destroy the Triqui people. Some insects are so important to them that they are woven into the Triqui's *huipiles*. Though each *huipil* has a white background and rows of red stripes, no two are alike. A red stripe is called an *oruga,* or caterpillar, and the colorful embroidery on it is called a *mariposa,* or butterfly. Because butterflies have so many colors and patterns, the women strive to make all these stripes unique. The middle panel is the broadest, prettiest, and most difficult to make. In its center, near the heart, is a wider stripe called the *figura madre,* the giver of life.

Mothers teach their daughters how to dye threads, operate the loom, sew, and embroider. A long time ago, thread was dyed using herbs, minerals, and flowers. The bright red dye for the *huipil* was produced using an insect called *grana cochinilla* found in cacti known as *nopales*. Nowadays women use industrialized cotton, acrylic yarn, and synthetic dyes. Most small Triqui communities now have at least one computer in their school, and some girls use it to design the *mariposas* they will embroider in their *huipil*.

A Triqui girl will say that her head rising out of the *huipil* is the sun; the design around her neck represents its rays; and the long ribbons that hang in the back symbolize the rain or the rainbows that the sun produces on a rainy

Glossary for "Ouch!"

abeja (ah-BEH-ha) [Spanish] bee

araña (ah-RAH-nyah) [Spanish] spider

avispa (ah-VEES-pah) [Spanish] wasp

guayaba (gwah-YAH-bah) [Spanish] guava, a tropical fruit

hormiga (orr-MEE-gah) [Spanish] ant

¡Lárgate! (LAR-gah-teh) [Spanish] Scram!

mamey (mah-MAY) [Spanish] a tropical fruit that is shaped like a small football with rough brown skin and sweet, coral/orange pulp

mariposa (mah-ree-POH-sah) [Spanish] butterfly

mosco (MOHS-coh) [Spanish] mosquito

piojo (pee-OH-hoh) [Spanish] louse

pulga (POOL-gah) [Spanish] flea

Glossary for "The Triqui"

figura madre (fee-GUH-rah MAH-dreh) [Spanish, "mother figure"] the middle stripe in a huipil from San Andrés Chicahuaxtla; see *huipil*

day. Combined, they signify the cycle of life, a constant process of change and renovation.

Sometimes women weave alone, and these silent times are used for contemplation. At other times they get together, each working on her own *huipil,* while gossiping, chatting, and sharing tales. These are moments for learning traditions and listening to stories like "Ouch!"

grana cochinilla (GRAH-nah koh-chee-NEE-yah) [Spanish] an insect that lives in *nopal* cacti and was once used to create the red dye that the Triqui used in making *huipiles;* the dye is still used today

huipil (wee-PEEL) [Spanish] an ankle-length, traditional, bright-red blouse worn by Triqui women; plural *huipiles* (wee-PEEL-ehs)

Mixteca (meeks-TEH-kah) [Spanish] the western part of Oaxaca where the Triqui live

nopal (noh-PAHL) [Spanish] a type of cactus also known as *opuntia* and paddle cactus

Oaxaca (wah-HA-kah) [Spanish] a state in Mexico

oruga (oh-RUH-gah) [Spanish] caterpillar

petate (peh-TAH-teh) [Spanish] a woven palm mat used by the Triquis for sleeping

San Andrés Chicahuaxtla (SAHN anh-DRES chee-kah-WUACS-tlah) [Spanish] a mountainous Triqui settlement

San Juan Copala (SAHN HUAHN koh-PAH-lah) [Spanish] a Triqui settlement in the low zone

Triqui (TREE-kee) [Triqui] native group that lives in the Mixteca; they call themselves "the people of the complete language"

A Tseltal Tale

Pokok Up High

The sky was blue. The sun was splendid. Pokok the frog's belly was full of flies and mosquitoes. His heart was so happy— BOOM, BOOM, BA BOOM!—that it danced in his chest.

He hopped over to say good-bye to his mother and grandmother.

His *mamá* asked, "Where are you going, *mi corazón*?"

"To swim," he answered.

"Be careful and come back soon, *cariño*," his *abuela* said.

When Pokok reached the pond, he dove into the water. He swam for a while, his legs pumping up and down. Then he flipped over, his belly standing out like an island. He stared at the clear sky.

He saw a small black spot up high. It circled down, closer and closer.

The spot turned out to be Xulem, the buzzard.

Xulem landed with a series of hops and skips. He shook his tail, tucked in his wings, and lurched to the edge of the pond.

"*Buenos días*, Pokok," he said.

"*Hola*, Xulem," Pokok answered. "Have you had a good morning?"

Xulem said, "I had a delightful breakfast. Now I'm thirsty, so I came down for a drink."

While Xulem drank, Pokok watched him. Xulem's bald head was ugly and spotted. His craggy beak was huge. His wrinkled neck was dirty. But the feathers of his magnificent wings gleamed in the sunlight.

Pokok sighed and said, "How lovely to be able to fly. I'm stuck on the ground and can only leap from place to place."

"Yes, flying is superb," Xulem said. "Poor Pokok, you have no idea how magnificent the world looks from up there."

"What do you see?" Pokok asked.

"I see mighty rivers, golden cornfields, and mountain peaks so high they are dressed in clouds," Xulem said. "I also see huge forests and lakes that reflect the sky."

He opened his wings and was about to take off when he saw Pokok's wistful gaze.

"Would you like to take a ride?" he asked.

"Yes!" Pokok said, so excited that his heart beat BOOM, BOOM, BA BOOM!

Xulem crouched, and Pokok jumped onto his back. He held on as best he could.

Xulem took off. He soared and glided in and out of clouds and even skimmed close to the ground. Pokok looked at the world spread out below him. He swiveled his head from side to side, left, right, left, right. He was so thrilled he felt his heart was going to fly out of his mouth . . . BOOM, BOOM, BA BOOM!

Then a strange odor reached his nose.

He sniffed . . .

And snuffled . . .

It came from Xulem's head. Pokok sniffed again and said, "I hate to mention this, but your head smells."

Xulem twisted his head and said, "Pokok, that is very rude!"

So Pokok kept quiet. For a while he enjoyed the view until the unpleasant aroma reached his nose once more.

He sniffed again and said, "Pardon me, Xulem, but your head really stinks!"

Xulem craned his neck and stared at Pokok so hard that the frog snapped his mouth shut.

Pokok tried to enjoy the view, but the terrible stench made its way to his nose. He blurted, "I'm sorry, Xulem, but your head reeks!"

Xulem shook himself hard.

Pokok started to slip off the buzzard's back.

"Help, help!" he yelled as he slithered off, clawing to get a hold.

His heart—BOOM, BOOM, BA BOOM!—was about to jump out of his mouth when, just in time, he clamped it shut.

Down, down, down he fell, past the clouds, past the mountain peaks, past the treetops . . . and he crashed, belly down, on the ground.

Whoosh! The air was knocked out of him.

There he lay, his hurt heart beating slower and slower and slower . . . boom, boom, ba boom . . . until his *mamá* and *abuela* found him.

"*¡Mi corazón!*" his *mamá* cried.

"*¡Pobrecito!*" his *abuela* said.

He was so happy to see them that his heart gave a little jump and then a skip. Little by little it beat harder and, after a while, it settled back to his chest.

Pokok's *mamá* and *abuela* carried him home. They nursed him as best they could, and soon he was almost his normal self. He was safely on the ground, and his heart was in its usual place. What more could he ask for?

Since that day no *xulem* has ever again given a *pokok* a ride on its back . . . and all *pokoks* have a flattened shape.

The Tseltal

The Tseltal, along with the Tsotsil, Chontal, Lacandón, and others, are descendants of the ancient Maya. Today the Tseltal are the largest native group in the southeastern state of Chiapas.

The *communidades* and small towns where the Tseltal live have cobblestone streets, homes painted in all the colors of the rainbow, and nearby fields of *maíz* and coffee. Some parts of Tseltal territory are high up in the mountains. In winter frequent fogs hide the trees and hills. Other areas of their communities are tropical, their jungles alive with frogs, buzzards, insects, birds, snakes, and elusive jaguars that live among the many unexplored pyramids and ruins that are hidden under the dense vegetation. Many of these animals often find themselves the subjects of Tseltal folktales.

The Tseltal live in family groups made up of parents, their children, and their children's spouses and children— much like Pokok's family. A *bankilal,* or elder brother, leads the group, having been chosen out of respect for his age and wisdom. He's in charge of managing the concerns of the family group and organizing its agricultural activities.

The Tseltal call themselves the *bats'il winik* and *bats'il ants,* meaning "true men" and "true women." Their language is called *Bats'il k'op,* or "the original word," and it sounds sweet and melodic. It's a language spoken from the heart. *O'tanil,* the heart, is so important to the Tseltals that they say, "The heart is us. Our hearts are me."

The word "heart" pops up in Tseltal conversations and stories all the time. If you see a giggling girl and ask her, "How are you?" she will probably answer, "My heart is happy." But if she is sad, she might say, "My heart hurts." If you bump into a boy who saw something scary, like a monster or an evil spirit, he'll say, "My heart escaped," just like Pokok's almost did as he fell to the earth. The Tseltal language is also a way of transmitting traditions and tales. There is an ancient belief that if *k'aal,* the sun, has a ring around it, it will gobble up all the delicious children it sees below. When some of the older people, their hearts beating hard, see a halo around the sun, they will shoo their grandkids into the house until the sun is back to normal.

The Tseltal love a *fiesta.* The elders work to ensure that all celebrations are happy occasions. The most famous religious celebration is Carnival. This *fiesta* is filled with music, dance, and color. During these traditional events, the women wear hand-woven and embroidered blouses and long skirts. The men wear vivid red clothing, including necklaces with coins that tinkle when they walk and dance. Red is also a favored color among the many bright ribbons that spring, like a fountain, from the top of the straw hats the men wear. The Tseltal love to make their hearts pound during this celebration. One *fiesta* activity involves chasing and catching a *torito de petate,* a bull made of woven mats and worn by a man.

The Tseltal also have agricultural celebrations. The land is of extreme importance to them. It's the place where everything begins and ends and where memory exists. *Maíz* is their

Glossary for "Pokok Up High"

abuela (ah-BWEH-lah) [Spanish] grandmother

buenos días (BWEH-nohs DEE-ahs) [Spanish] good morning

cariño (kah-REE-nyoh) [Spanish] sweetheart; can also be used as a synonym for love

hola (oh-LAH) [Spanish] hello

mamá (mah-MAH) [Spanish] mother

¡Mi corazón! (MEE koh-rah-SOHN) [Spanish] My heart!, a term of endearment

¡Pobrecito! (poh-breh-SEE-toh) [Spanish] Poor thing!

pokok (poh-KOHK) [Bats'il k'op] frog

xulem (shoo-LEM) [Bats'il k'op] buzzard

Glossary for "The Tseltal"

(The ' found in some of the pronunciations listed below stands for a short pause, as in "uh-oh.")

bankilal (ban-kee-LAHL) [Bats'il k'op] elder

44

most important crop, and children help to plant and harvest it. Not even one grain will be misused, because the Tseltal believe that they are what they eat. According to legend, the gods made the first humans—those who have hearts and souls—out of corn. Planting *maíz* is a sacred activity—besides feeding the family, it feeds the gods.

Because of this, the Tseltal believe that without the land they are nothing.

Like Pokok, who lives on the ground, the soil is where the Tseltal nurture their hearts and roots.

bats'il ants (bats'EEL ANTS) [Bats'il k'op] true women

Bats'il k'op (Bats'EEL K'OHP) [Bats'il k'op, "the true word"] language spoken by the Tseltal

bats'il winik (Bats'EEL VEE-neek) [Bats'il k'op] true men

Chontal (chon-TAHL) [Spanish] descendants of the Maya

communidades (koh-moo-knee-DAH-des) [Spanish] communities

fiesta (fee-EHS-tah) [Spanish] party or celebration

k'aal (k'AHL) [Bats'il k'op] the sun

Lacandón (lah-can-DOHN) [Spanish] descendants of the Maya

maíz (my-EES) [Spanish] corn

Maya (MY-yah) [Spanish] ancient native group of Mexico

o'tanil (oh'tan-EEL) [Bats'il k'op] heart

torito de petate (tor-EE-toh DEH peh-TAH-teh) [Spanish] bull costume made of woven mats

Tseltal (tsel-TAHL) [Spanish] descendants of the Maya

Tsotsil (Tsoht-SEEL) [Spanish] descendants of the Maya

Conclusion

Where else in the world will you find a clever cricket who defeats a puma, a patient turtle who helps to create the world, a brave opossum who gives mankind a wonderful gift, a flea who saves humanity, and a frog who, just in time, keeps his heart in his chest?

Only in Mexico!

Yet every culture in the world has tales that are important to its people. Like the stories in this book, all fairy tales and folktales allow people to pass along traditions and knowledge not only among their own community, but also to the world. Through stories we come to understand ourselves as well as the world around us. Perhaps the tales in *Whiskers, Tails & Wings* will encourage you to share your own stories, discover new tales, and maybe even create your own!

Bibliography

Acuña Delgado, Ángel. "Correr para vivir: El dilema Rarámuri." *Desacato—Revista en Antropología Social*, no. 12 (Fall 2003), 130–46: **http://redalyc.uaemex.mx/redalyc/pdf/139/13901210.pdf**. Offers information about resistance and long-distance running among the Tarahumara.

———"Análisis estructural y valor de la resistencia en la carrera rarámuri de la Sierra Tarahumara." *Dimensión Antropológica* 27, (February–May 2003): **http://www.dimensionantropologica.inah.gob.mx/?p=877**. Provides information about long-distance running.

Aguilera García, María del Carmen. *Flora y fauna mexicana—Mitología y tradiciones.* Mexico City: Editorial Everest Mexicana, n.d.

Apodaca, Paul. "Cactus Stones: Symbolism and Representation in Southern California and Seri Indigenous Folk Art and Artifacts." *Journal of California and Great Basin Anthropology* 23, no. 2, (2001): 215–228: **http://www.clas.ufl.edu/users/davidson/Archaeology%20Lab%20Material%20Culture/Week%206%20Nature%20of%20artifacts/2001,%20Apodaca,%20cogged%20stones%20of%20california.pdf**. An article about different cacti in the Seri region and how cacti impact the Seri's lives.

Aranda T., Flor de María, ed. "El mundo mixteco y zapoteco." *México desconocido* (1993), no.12. A guide to Mexican tourism, this magazine and website (**http://www.mexicodesconocido.com.mx**) offers information on the country's history, culture, natural history, festivals, and food.

Balderrama García, Bernardo, Christian Heeb, and Andrew Hudson. *Copper Canyon*. San Diego, CA: Photo Tour Books, 2009.

Beauregard, Art. "Running Feet." Term paper, December 1996: **http://www.lehigh.edu/~dmd1/art.html**. Offers information on ultramarathon running and the Tarahumara, with additional details about their way of life.

Bermejo, Juan Manuel. "Huicholes, artesanos místicos (Nayarit)." *México desconocido* 338, (April 2005): **http://www.mexicodesconocido.com.mx/huicholes-artesanos-misticos-nayarit.html**. An article about Huichol folk art.

Borja Aguirre, Daniel. "El maíz" paper: **http://www.monografias.com/ trabajos/elmaiz/elmaiz.shtml**. Presents information about corn and its history, development, and varieties.

Coronado Martínez, Elva. "Somos mujeres mariposas—Retrato femenino de un mundo simbólico." *El caracol*, no. 2 (July–September 2006): 12–13: **http://www.culturaspopulareseindigenas.gob.mx/pdf/CARACOL_2.pdf**. Explains how *huipiles* are made.

De Orellana, Margarita, ed. "Textiles de Chiapas." Special issue, *Artes de México*, 1993.

———"Textiles de Oaxaca." Special issue, *Artes de México*, 1996.

———"Arte huichol." Special issue, *Artes de México*, 2005.

———"Mitos del maíz." Special issue, *Artes de México*, 2006.

———"Rituales del maíz." Special issue, *Artes de México*, 2006.

"Enfrentan nulas ventas tejedoras de huipiles triques." *Correo mixteco* (November 30, 2007): **http://correomixteco.com/noticias/enfrentan-nulas-ventas-tejedoras-de-huipiles-triquis.htm** (*huipiles*). An article detailing the decline of *huipil* sales and how this affects weavers and the Triqui economy in general.

Flores, Alejandra. "Arte wixarica, tradición y color/Wixarica Folk Art, Tradition and Color." *Vive México* (December 2007–February 2008), 37–48.

Gómez Muñoz, Maritza. *Tzeltales*. Mexico City: Comisión Nacional para el Desarrollo de los Pueblo Indígenas (CDI) / Programa de las Naciones Unidas para el Desarrollo (PNUD), 2004.

González, Refugio. *Soy huichol*. Mexico City: Secretaría de Educación Pública (SEP), Libros del Rincón, [1988] 1995.

"Grupos étnicos de Sonora, los seri." *Como México no hay dos*, posted by Isaac, September 14, 2008: **http://charritomex.multiply.com/journal/item/73/73**. Offers historical information about the Seri.

Herrero, Adrián. "Los huicholes." *En fuga*: **http://culturasdelatierra.blogspot. com/2010/12/los-huicholes_07.html**. Provides information about the Huichol and their spiritual beliefs.

Ibarra Martínez, Obdulia, and Teresa Blanco Moreno. *Sin maíz no hay juego-entretenimientos*. Mexico City: Consejo Nacional para la Cultura y las Artes (CONACULTA) / Dirección General de Culturas Populares e Indígenas, 2004.

"Isla del Tiburón, la más grande del septentrión" in "Tips de Aeroméxico." *México desconocido* 6 (Winter 1997–1998): **http://www.mexicodesconocido. com.mx.isla-del-tiburon-la-mas-grande-del-septentrion.html**. Gives information about Isla Tiburón.

Jiménez, Arturo (article), and José Carlo González (photos). "La nación seri, un paraíso calcinante de desierto, mar, cultura y autonomía." *La jornada*: **http://www.jornada.unam.mx/reportajes/?id=seris**. An article about the Seri and the challenges they face.

Johnson, Bernice. "Face Painting," in *The Seri Indians of Sonora Mexico*. Tucson, Arizona: University of Arizona Press, 1970: **http://www.uapress.arizona. edu/onlinebks/SERIS/PAINT.HTM**. Provides photos of and information about Seri face paint.

"Las danzas, la unión entre la realidad y el misticismo (danza del venado y danza del pascola." *Vive Mazatlán*: **http://www.vivemazatlan.com/ index.php/Click-para-ver-el-tema-de-su-interes/Las-danzas-la-union- entre-la-realidad-y-el-misticismo.html**. An article about the pascola dance and its mysticism.

Lazcano Sandoval, Carlos. "Barrancas del Cobre, el sistema barranqueño más grande del mundo, en Chihuahua." *México desconocido*: **http://www.mexicodesconocido.com.mx/barrancas-del-cobre-el-sis- tema-barranqueno-mas-grande-del-mundo.html**. Lewin Fischer, Pedro, and Fausto Sandoval Cruz. *Triquis*. Mexico City: CDI, 2007.

Luque Agraz, Diana, and Antonio Robles Torres. *Naturalezas, saberes y territorios comcaác (seri): diversidad cultural y sustentabilidad ambiental*. Mexico City: Secretaría de Medio Ambiente y Recursos Naturales (SEMARNAT) - Instituto Nacional de Ecología (INE) - Centro de Investigación en Alimentación y Desarrollo, A.C. 2006: **http://books.google.com.mx/books?id=2rtZh- StP61IC**. Gives information about the Seri and their knowledge about the plants and animals that live in their area.

Maldonado Ortiz, Carlos. "Punta Chueca, un refugio seri en Sonora." *México desconocido* 239 (January 1997): **http://www.mexicodesconocido.com.mx/ punta-chueca-un-refugio-seri-en-sonora.html**. A first-person report about the Seri and their way of life.

Méndez, Elízabeth. "El encuentro con el espíritu del híkuri (peyote)." *Real de Catorce*: **http://www.realdecatorce.net/huicholes.htm**. An explanation of the importance of peyote to the Huichol.

Nabhan, Gary Paul. *Singing the Turtles to Sea: The Comcáac (Seri) Art and Science of Reptiles*: **http://books.google.com.mx/books?id=HLSboGisPXQC**. Provides information about sea turtles and their importance to the Seri.

Neurath, Johannes. *Huicholes*. Mexico City: CDI / PNUD, 2003.

Ortíz Garay, Andrés. "Pascola, el viejo de la fiesta, Sinaloa." *México desconocido* 287 (January 2001): **http://www.mexicodesconocido.com.mx/pascola-el-viejo-de-la-fiesta-Sinaloa**. Article about the pascola and its importance to the native groups that live in northern Mexico.

Pintado, Cortina, and Ana Paula. *Tarahumaras*. Mexico City: CDI / PNUD, 2003.

Rabchinskey, Ilán, and Regina Tattersfield. *Yo' tan k'op-Corazón de la palabra*. Mexico City: Trilce, Instituto Nacional de Antropología e Historia (INAH), Instituto Nacional de Lenguas Indígenas (INALI) - Fondo Nacional para la Cultura y las Artes (FONCA), 2009.

Rentería, Valencia, and Rodrigo Fernando. *Seris*. Mexico City: CDI, 2007.

Robledo, Hernández, and Gabriela P. *Los tarahumaras*. Mexico City: Instituto Nacional Indigenista (INI), 1981.

Romero, Roberto. "Viaje al Río Tulijá, corazón tzeltal en Chiapas." *México desconocido*, 366 (April 2007): **http://www.mexicodesconocido.com.mx/viaje-al-rio-tulija-corazon-tzeltal-en-chiapas.html**. An article about the natural beauty of three areas where the Tseltal live.

Sarmiento Pradera, Manuel, ed. "Herbolaria Mexicana." Special guide, *México desconocido*, no. 4–6, n.d.

Takahashi, Masako. *Textiles mexicanos*. Mexico City: Noriega Editores, 2003.

Triedo, Nicolás. "Viaje a Wirikuta. La tierra del peyote, la morada de todos los dioses (Nayarit)." *México desconocido* 233 (July 1996): **http://www.mexicodesconocido.com.mx/viaje-a-wirikuta.-la-tierra-del-peyote-la-morada-de-todos-los-dioses.html**. An article about the Huichols' sacred pilgrimage to Wirikuta, in San Luis Potosí.

Vela, Enrique, ed. "Alucinógenos del México prehispánico." Special issue, *Arqueología mexicana* 10, no. 59 (January–February 2003).

———"El maíz." Special issue, *Arqueología mexicana* 5, no. 25 (May–June 1997).

———"Las culturas de Sonora—Entre el mar y el cielo." Special issue, *Arqueología mexicana* 17, no. 97 (May–June 2009).

———"Plantas medicinales prehispánicas." Special issue, *Arqueología mexicana* 7, no. 39 (September–October 1999).

———"Textiles del México de ayer y de hoy." Special issue, *Arqueología mexicana*, no. 19 (September–October 2005).

Wirrárika. Zapopan, Jalisco, Mexico: Wirrárika Huichol Ethnographic Museum, 2008.

Web Resources

CIESAS. (Centro de Investigaciones y Estudios Superiores en Antropología Social) Perfil indígena, tarahumaras

http://pacificosur.ciesas.edu.mx/perfilindigena/tarahumaras/conte11.html

A website dedicated to the social anthropology of the Tarahumara.

CIESAS, Tzeltales de Chiapas

http://pacificosur.ciesas.edu.mx/fichas/opcion26.html

A website dedicated to the social anthropology of the Tseltal.

Comisión Nacional para el Desarrollo de los Pueblos Indígenas (CDI.), Mexico.

http://www.cdi.gob.mx

Accesses PDF files pertaining to all the native groups of Mexico.

Grupo tortuguero comcaác

http://gtc-seri.blogspot.com

Information about turtles and what the Seri are doing to protect them and their eggs.

Huicholes, RED ILCE (Instituto Latinoamericano de la Comunicación Educativa)

http://redescolar.ilce.edu.mx/redescolar/publicaciones/publi_mexico/publihuicholes.htm

Provides information for children about the Huichol.

ILV/SIL México

http://pnglanguages.org/mexico/

The Summer Institute of Linguistics' site provides Mexican language resources.

Instituto Lingüístico de Verano, Triqui de San Juan Copala

http://www.sil.org/MEXICO/mixteca/triqui-copala/00e-TriquiCopala-trc.htm

The Instituto Lingüístico de Verano site offers information about Triqui language, folklore, and customs.

Instituto Nacional de Lenguas Indígenas

http://www.inali.gob.mx

Offers information about the different languages spoken by the indigenous people of Mexico.

Mexico/Seris. RED ILCE (Instituto Latinoamericano de la Comunicación Educativa)

http://redescolar.ilce.edu.mx/redescolar/publicaciones/publi_mexico/publiseris.htm

Provides information for children about the Seri.

Popularte-mayense-tzeltales

http://www.uv.mx/Popularte/Esp/scriptphp.php?sid=19

Provides information about the Tseltal.

Running with the Tarahumara

http://www.studyspanish.com/comps/running2.htm

A first-person account of a marathon runner who ran with the Tarahumara.

Southwest Agave Project, "The Tarahumara"

http://www.ic.arizona.edu/~agave/ceram_feast_tarah01.htm

Provides information about *tesgüino*.

Tarahumaras o rarámuris, RED ILCE (Instituto Latinoamericano de la Comunicación Educativa)

http://redescolar.ilce.edu.mx/redescolar/publicaciones/publi_mexico/publitarahumaras.htm

Provides information for children about the Tarahumara.

Triquis de Oaxaca-Nanj nïn ïn

http://www.triquis.org/

Offers information about the Triqui.

Triquis, RED ILCE (Instituto Latinoamericano de la Comunicación Educativa)

http://redescolar.ilce.edu.mx/redescolar/publicaciones/publi_mexico/publitriqui.htm

Provides information for children about the Triqui.

Tzeltales

http://www.semarnat.gob.mx/presenciainternacional/fronterasur/Paginas/Tzeltales.aspx

Secretaría de Medio Ambiente y Recursos Naturales (SEMARNAT) website that offers information about the Tseltal.

Tzeltales, RED ILCE (Instituto Latinoamericano de la Comunicación Educativa)

http://www.redescolar.ilce.edu.mx/redescolar/publicaciones/publi_mexico/publitzeltzales.htm

Provides information for children about the Tseltal.

Tale Sources

Tarahumara

Anonymous. "El general grillo—Cuento chontal," in *De aluxes, estrellas, animales y otros relatos—Cuentos indígenas*. Mexico City: Secretaría de Educación Pública (SEP), Libros del Rincón, Colección Zenzontle, 1991.

Cueto, Mireya, Magali Martínez, Luis de la Peña, and Armida de la Vara. "El tigre y el grillo," in *Cuéntame lo que se cuenta*. Mexico City: Consejo Nacional de Fomento Educativo (CONAFE), [1987] 1990.

González Casanova, Pablo. "El león y el grillo," in *Cuentos indígenas.* Mexico City: Universidad Nacional Autónoma de México (UNAM), [1946] 1965.

Laughlin, Robert M. "War Between the Cricket and the Jaguar," in *The People of the Bat: Mayan Tales and Dreams from Zinacantán*, edited by Carol Karasik. Washington, DC: Smithsonian Institution Press, 1988.

Radin, Paul. "El león y el grillo," in "Folktales from Oaxaca." Special edition, *Journal of American Folklore* 28 (1915).

Scheffler, Lilian. "El grillo y el león," in *Cuentos y leyendas de México*. Mexico City: Panorama Editorial, [1991] 1994.

Warner Giddings, Ruth. "The Cricket and the Lion," in *Yaqui Myths and Legends*. Tucson, Arizona: Anthropological Papers of the University of Arizona, 1959.

Seri

Delgado Sánchez, Gustavo. *La tierra de arena*. Mexico City: CONAFE, [1993] 2005.

Morales Colosio, Jesús. "La leyenda de la caguama," in *Relatos guarijíos—Nawe-sari makwrawi*, compiled by Lucila Mondragón. Lenguas de México, no. 7, Mexico City: CONACULTA / Dirección de Culturas Populares, 1995.

Olmos Aguilera, Miguel. "La leyenda de la caguama," in *El viejo, el venado y el coyote—Estética y cosmología*. Tijuana: El Colegio de la Frontera Norte; Mexicali: Fondo Regional para la Cultura y las Artes del Noroeste, 2005.

Huichol

Benítez, Fernando, from the story told by Aurelio Kánare. "Cómo el tlacuache pudo robarse el fuego," in *Cómo surgieron los seres y las cosas*, compiled by Martha Muñoz de Coronado. Venezuela: Coedición Latinoamericana, 1986.

Campos, Julieta. "Leyenda del fuego," in *La herencia obstinada: Análisis de cuentos nahuas*. Mexico City: Fondo de Cultura Económica, 1982.

López Austin, Alfredo. *Los mitos del tlacuache*. Mexico City: Alianza Editorial, 1990.

Taggart, James M. "Huitzilán versión 2," in *Nahuat Myth and Social Structure*, 103–4. Austin, Texas: University of Texas Press, 1983.

Triqui

Hollenbach, Elena E. de. "El mundo animal entre los triques," in *Tlalocan* 8 (1980), 437–490. See esp. tales 6.2 and 8.1.

Laughlin, Robert M. *Of Cabbages and Kings: Tales from Zinacantán*. Washington, D.C.: Smithsonian Institution Press, 1977. See esp. footnote of "Tale 54," p. 328.

Tseltal

Campos, Julieta. "La rana y el zopilote—Cuento nahua" *De aluxes, estrellas, animales y otros relatos—Cuentos indígenas*. Mexico City: SEP, Libros del Rincón, Colección Zenzontle, 1991.

Henestrosa, Andrés. "La tortuga—Cuento zapoteco" *De aluxes, estrellas, animales y otros relatos—Cuentos indígenas*. Mexico City: SEP, Libros del Rincón, Colección Zenzontle, 1991.

Cruz Ortíz, Alejandro. "El zopilote y la tortuga" (told by Margarita López of San Andrés Huaxpaltepec), in *Yakua kuia—El nudo del tiempo—Mitos y leyendas de la tradición oral mixteca*. Mexico City: Centro de Investigaciones y Estudios Superiores en Antropología Social (CIESAS), 1998.

"El zopilote y la tortuga," told by Lorenzo Cano Simón, 13-year-old Mixteco from Arroyo Faisán, San Luis Acatlán, Guerrero, in *Cuentos de engaños, para hacer reír y fantásticos*. Mexico City: CONAFE, 2001.

"El sapo y el zopilote," in *Sts 'unbal jts' ibtik, Sts'unobal jts'ibtik—Nuestras semillas literarias—Cuentos infantiles*. Chiapas, Mexico: Sna Jtz'ibajom, Cultura de los Indios Mayas, A.C., 2003.

Rabchinskey, Ilán, and Regina Tattersfield. *Yo' tan k'op-Corazón'de la palabra*. Mexico City: Trilce, INAH, INALI, FONCA, 2009.

Index